WEREWOLF MOON

PHASES OF THE MOON

The Full Moon
Seen from Earth

BY JULIANA HANFORD
ILLUSTRATED BY CARY PILLO

Kane Press
New York

To my best friend, Sarah—J.H.

To Jim—C.P.

Acknowledgments: Our thanks to Brian Abbott, Hayden Planetarium & American Museum of Natural History, for helping us make this book as accurate as possible.

Werewolf Moon is based on a premise by Susanna Pitzer.

Text copyright © 2009 by Kane Press, Inc.
Illustrations copyright © 2009 by Cary Pillo

Library of Congress Cataloging-in-Publication Data

Hanford, Juliana.
  Werewolf moon / by Juliana Hanford ; illustrated by Cary Pillo.
    p. cm. — (Science solves it!)
  "Earth Science/Phases of the Moon-Grades: 1/3 ."
  Summary: As Jake tries to find out if his bearded neighbor is really a werewolf, he learns about the phases of the moon.
  ISBN 978-1-57565-291-7 (alk. paper)
  [1. Moon—Fiction. 2. Werewolves—Fiction.] I. Pillo, Cary, ill. II. Title.
  PZ7.H1942We 2009
  [E]—dc22
                  2008049801

eISBN 978-1-57565-621-2

10 9 8 7 6 5 4 3

First published in the United States of America in 2009 by Kane Press, Inc.
Printed in China

Science Solves It! is a registered trademark of Kane Press, Inc.

Book Design: Edward Miller

Visit us online at **www.kanepress.com**

 Like us on Facebook
facebook.com/kanepress

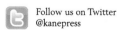 Follow us on Twitter
@kanepress

I'm frozen in my movie theater seat. It's not because my feet are glued to the sticky floor—even though they are. It's because I just saw the scariest movie ever made. *Attack of the Werewolf.*

I look over at my best friend, Stan.

"Jake," he says. "Let's get out of here!"

We meet my big sister, Angie, in the lobby.
She grins. "You guys seem a little freaked out.
I guess the wolf-man was scary?"

I try to look cool. "Whatever. I know
werewolves aren't *real*."

"Not real?" Angie stares at me. "Come on, kiddo. I thought you were smarter than that."

"I am smarter than that!" I say. "I mean . . . wait, what are you talking about?"

GLOW-IN-THE-DARK?
Our Moon is a big ball of rock that circles Earth. The Moon looks like it glows, but it really has no light of its own. It's just lit up by the Sun!

As we step outside, Angie looks up. There's a half moon in the big, black sky.

"Don't worry," she says. "You're safe tonight. Werewolves only attack when the moon is full."

Stan groans. "Angie, stop playing around."

"Hey, I'm just trying to keep you guys from getting *eaten*," she says. "Don't you know werewolves have been around forever? Since ancient times. And they can look just like regular people, so *anybody* could be one. Even your own next-door n—" She breaks off.

"Huh?" I ask. "Next-door . . . neighbor?"

"Now, Jake, don't flip out," she says. "But last week Mr. Ray moved in next door, right?" I nod.

Angie whispers, "Well, have you seen him lately? His beard is getting big and bushy— like *fur*. And every night he's out in his yard, staring at the moon. . . ."

8

"*Wha—?*" I say. But we've reached our house, and Angie strolls in without another word. Stan and I are about to follow, when we hear—

"Hi, kids!" It's my grandma. She lives across the street. "How was the scary movie?"

"Scary!" I shout.

She blows me a kiss and goes inside.

I SEE THE MOON
When you can see the Moon's whole bright side, it looks like a big ball. When you can see only a little of the Moon's bright side, it looks like a tiny sliver.

HALF AND HALF
In this picture you can only see half of the sunlit side of the Moon.

Then we hear a new voice. "Hello, boys!"
Mr. Ray is out in his yard—just like Angie said!
"Nice moon," he says. "Of course, nothing beats a full moon. You know, some folks say a full moon makes your blood run strong. Amazing, huh? It almost makes me feel young again!"
I look at Stan. We turn and dash inside.

"Dude!" says Stan. "Your neighbor is
totally a werewolf!"

"That whole moon-blood thing was creepy."
I shiver. "And his beard does look kind of furry."

Stan nods. "And the werewolf in the movie
felt young and strong, just like Mr. Ray said."

"Oh, man. Angie is right!" I say. "I live next
door to a *werewolf*! We need a plan."

The next weekend we hit the library. First we try to figure out when the full moon is coming. I find a moon chart. "Tonight's the *new moon*," I say. "That means you can't see the moon at all."

Stan gulps. "So after tonight it'll start looking bigger. And in two weeks, it'll be full!"

NO MOON—OR NEW MOON?

A new moon happens when the whole sunlit side of the Moon is facing away from Earth. Then the side facing us is totally dark—so we can't see the Moon at all.

The Moon's phases happen because of how the Sun shines on it as it circles around Earth.

Earth

Sun

Moon

We quickly look for anything that can stop a werewolf. "Here's something!" I point. "Wolfsbane—a flowering plant from the buttercup family. Keeps away werewolves!"

We go straight to the flower shop.

"Excuse me," I say to the guy behind the counter. "Do you have any wolfsbane?"

He looks at me like I have daffodils coming out my nose.

On our way home Stan says, "Silver bullets!
One book said they stop werewolves."

I roll my eyes. "We can't shoot Mr. Ray."

"I know *that*. But we could put something
silver near him and see if he acts weird."

Hmm. "My grandma has silver candlesticks,"
I say.

A few days later I'm at Grandma's. "May I use your candlesticks?" I ask. "I'm, uh, having a party. A really . . . fancy one."

"How nice!" she says. "You can have them all week, dear. I'll be away at my Green Gardens meeting. And guess what? Mr. Ray offered to take care of my plants for me. Isn't he a peach?"

"Yeah," I say. "A real . . . peach."

Outside, Mr. Ray is working in his yard. He looks more like a werewolf every day. His hair is bushy. His beard is bushy. Even his eyebrows are bushy.

And the moon is already a bright sliver in the sky.

DID YOU KNOW?
After the new moon, the Moon seems to be getting bigger. Then it is called a **waxing** moon. When it seems to be getting smaller, it is called a **waning** moon.

Later that week, Stan and I spot Mr. Ray
napping in his hammock. We creep over. "Now
what?" I say.

Stan whispers, "Put the candlesticks on him."

"You mean just throw them in the hammock?
What if he wakes up? What if he *wolfs out?*"

YAWN. Mr. Ray's eyelids flutter open. We're
dead meat.

"Hi, boys," he says, blinking. "Say, aren't those your Grandma Gertie's candlesticks?"

I open my mouth, but no words come out. *How does he know that?*

Then Mr. Ray says, "Jake, let me ask you something. Has your grandma . . . said anything to you? About me, I mean?"

"Uh—about you?" I squeak.

"Yes. She hasn't . . . *mentioned* anything?"

"Um. Just that you're watering her plants."

"Oh." He breathes out a little sigh. "Okay."

We turn to leave. But then Mr. Ray says, "It's a half moon tonight. If your grandma calls, tell her I'm watching it." He smiles slowly. "She'll be back when it's full, you know."

WAX ON, WAX OFF
How can you tell whether the Moon is waxing or waning? When the half moon looks like the letter D, it's waxing. When the half moon looks like a backwards letter D, it's waning.

Stan and I rush inside my house.

"Wow," Stan says. "Your grandma is in major trouble! Mr. Ray is going to make a midnight snack out of her!"

"He can try," I say. "But he'll have to get through me first."

We decide to keep a stakeout on Mr. Ray. Every afternoon we watch him dig up weeds in my grandma's garden.

Every night we watch him stand in his yard and stare at the moon. It gets fuller and fuller.

Finally the big night is here. Stan and I are looking at the bright, round moon when Grandma gets home. Mr. Ray is waiting for her. But instead of crossing the street, he ducks into his garden shed.

"Quick!" says Stan. "Now's our chance!"

FULL MOON

When the Moon is full, we can see the whole side of it that is lit up by the Sun. Some legends say the full moon makes people act oddly, but most scientists say those are just stories.

We run next door. My heart is racing. My
palms are sweating. I think I might faint.

SLAM! We close the door behind Mr. Ray
and flip the latch. Phew!

Bang-bang-bang. "Boys! Boys? Hey, open up!"

Then Grandma marches over. "What on earth do you think you're doing?"

"We're trying to save you!" I say. Behind me, Mr. Ray is still *bang-bang-banging* on the door.

Grandma frowns. "Save me from what?"

"From Mr. Ray!" I cry. "He's a werewolf!"

The banging stops. There's dead silence.

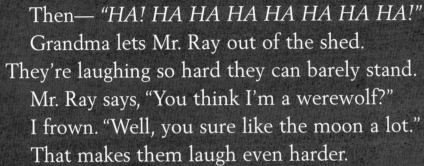

Then— *"HA! HA HA HA HA HA HA HA!"*
Grandma lets Mr. Ray out of the shed.
They're laughing so hard they can barely stand.
Mr. Ray says, "You think I'm a werewolf?"
I frown. "Well, you sure like the moon a lot."
That makes them laugh even harder.

"Boys," says Grandma. "Mr. Ray is teaching me to garden by the phases of the moon. Some people from my meeting think it really works!"

"Oh. But why all that *full* moon stuff?" I ask.

Grandma blushes. "Well, Mr. Ray and I made a date to go gardening under the full moon."

"Oh," I say again. "A date." Wait. *"A date?"*

Grandma smiles. "That's why Larry went into his shed—to get his gardening tools."

"So . . . the beard isn't werewolf fur?" I ask.

Mr. Ray grins. "Your grandma said she loves a nice full beard. She told me I look like a sea captain—sailing his ship by moonlight!"

Grandma blushes harder this time.

"*Oh,*" I say. "Right. Okay, then! You guys have fun gardening. Um, good night!"

Stan and I can still hear them laughing as we head for my house.

Inside, we hear someone else laughing.

It's Angie. I glare at her. "Why did you tell us Mr. Ray was a werewolf?"

She grins. "Sorry, kiddo. After that movie, I just couldn't resist! Besides, he *is* kind of furry."

I shrug. "Well, that's true."

Stan gives me a nudge. "I think your grandma and Mr. Ray are kind of cute together."

I look out the window. Mr. Ray is handing Grandma a flower from his moon garden.

I smile a little to myself. You know, they are kind of cute. Maybe Mr. Ray is okay after all. And hey, at least he's not a werewolf!

WHAT HAPPENS AFTER A FULL MOON?

The whole cycle starts over! The Moon will go from a full moon to a new moon and back to full again. And people on Earth will continue to watch the changing Moon, just as we always have!

WE CAN INVESTIGATE!

AWHOOOOOOO!

THINK LIKE A SCIENTIST

Scientists are like ace detectives. They gather evidence and look for clues that will help them solve a mystery—a *science* mystery! Scientists observe, collect information, and test out their ideas. They *investigate*!

Look Back
- On page 12, what is the first thing Jake and Stan investigate? What do they find out?
- What do they investigate on page 13? What do they think of on 15? How do they try to test their ideas?

Try This!
Do a Moon experiment! You need: a flashlight, a ball (or something round, like an orange), and a buddy.
- Hold up the ball. Pretend it is the Moon.
- Have your partner stand still and shine a flashlight on the ball. Your partner is the Sun.
- *You* are the Earth! Stand in one place and slowly start to turn around (just like the rotating Earth). As you turn, look at how the light and shadows change on the Moon. This is how the Moon's phases happen!

The girl sees the new moon phase.

The girl sees the full moon phase.